First Little Readers™

Biggy the Bunny

by Liza Charlesworth

ISBN: 978-1-338-29793-5

Illustrated by Tammie Lyon

First printing, June 2018.

Hi! My name is Benny.
This is a picture of my bunny.

My bunny is very, very, very,
very, very . . .

BIG!

My bunny is bigger than my house.
That is why I named her Biggy.

Biggy likes to eat.
She eats 1,000 carrots each day.
CRUNCH! CRUNCH! CRUNCH!

Biggy likes to drink.
She drinks all the water
in my pool.

Biggy likes to play hide and seek.
She is very easy to spot!
Do you see her?

Biggy likes to dress up.
She is Benny!
I am Biggy!

Biggy likes to race.
One, two, three, go!

I run as fast as I can . . .

but Biggy always wins.

Biggy likes to give me rides.
We go all around town.

HOP, HOP, HOP!

She gives my friends rides, too.
HOP, HOP, HOP!

Taking care of Biggy
is a lot of work.
But it is so worth it.

My big bunny is the very, very, very, very, very BEST!